the 3 bears
and Goldilocks

For Chloë—M. W.

For my friends Shay and Tristin Michael—H. M. S.

Atheneum Books for Young Readers
An imprint of Simon & Schuster Children's Publishing Division
1230 Avenue of the Americas, New York, New York 10020
Text copyright © 2008 by Margaret Willey
Illustrations copyright © 2008 by Heather M. Solomon
All rights reserved, including the right of reproduction in whole or in part in any form.
Book design by Sonia Chaghatzbanian
The text for this book is set in Electra.
The illustrations for this book are rendered in watercolor, collage, color pencils, acrylic, and oil paint.
Manufactured in China
First Edition
2 4 6 8 10 9 7 5 3 1
Library of Congress Cataloging-in-Publication Data
Willey, Margaret.
The 3 Bears and Goldilocks / Margaret Willey ; illustrated by Heather M. Solomon. — 1st ed.
p. cm.
Summary: Goldilocks, ignoring her father's warning not to rush in where she does not belong, enters a cabin in the
woods, cleans it to meet her standards, plucks from the porridge items unappealing to her before eating a bowlful,
and falls asleep on the bed that suits her best.
ISBN-13: 978-1-4169-2494-4
ISBN-10: 1-4169-2494-9
[1. Behavior—Fiction. 2. Bears—Fiction. 3. Self-actualization
(Psychology)—Fiction.]
I. Solomon, Heather, ill. II. Title. III. Title: The Three Bears and Goldilocks.
PZ7.W65548Aac 2008
[E]—dc22
2007013857

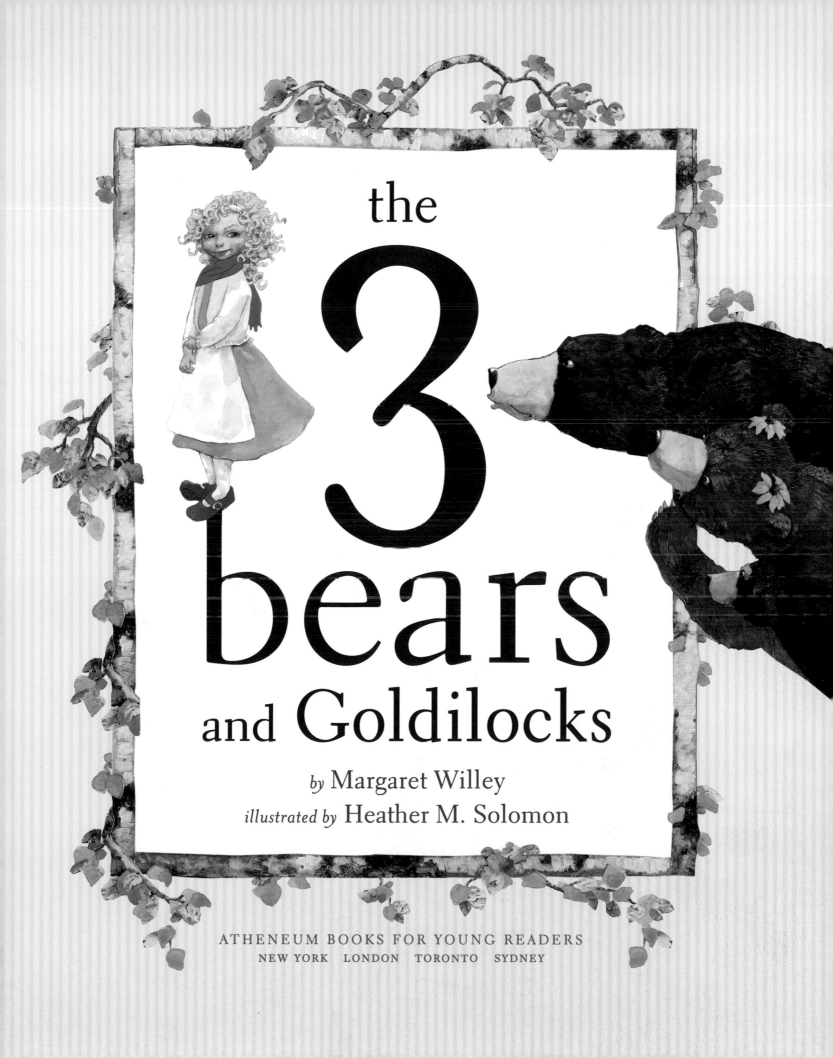

the 3 bears

and Goldilocks

by Margaret Willey

illustrated by Heather M. Solomon

ATHENEUM BOOKS FOR YOUNG READERS
NEW YORK LONDON TORONTO SYDNEY

In the farthest reaches of the far north lived a girl named Goldilocks, who was bolder than most and very curious.

One morning her father wrapped a bright scarf around her neck
and said, "It is all very well to love adventure, child, but you must be
careful not to rush headlong into places where you don't belong."

And Goldilocks listened, but did not *really* listen.

She set off by herself into the forest to see what amusements she might find.

She went along and she went along, down a twisting path through tall pines and firs and junipers, until she came to a sunny clearing with no trees—only a small cabin with a heavy door.

Goldilocks was too curious to walk past. She thought,
I will go up to the door and knock three times and see if whoever
is inside might invite me to play.

She knocked
once,
twice,
three times.

No one answered, but the door
opened slightly—just enough for
Goldilocks to see into the room
beyond. It was a room unlike any
room she had ever seen! The floor
was strewn from corner to corner
with leaves and berry stems and
pine cones and fish bones and
thick, brown fur.

No one could play in this messy place, Goldilocks thought. She took a raggedy broom from behind the door and began to sweep, thinking that her mother would be very proud of her for being so helpful. She swept for a long time, until the floors were clear and the pile of sweepings outside the cabin door was waist-high.

All of that work made her very hungry, so she looked about the cabin for something to eat. Near the hearth were three bowls of still-warm porridge, but it was unlike any porridge that Goldilocks had ever seen! It was mixed with beetles, bark, lumps of grass, and fish scales.

What awful porridge these forest folk eat, Goldilocks thought. But she was so hungry that she picked through all of the lumps in the smallest bowl, sweetened what was left with honey from a honey jar, and ate every last bite.

All of that porridge made Goldilocks very tired, and she looked about herself for a comfortable place to rest. In a room at the back of the cabin there were three beds, but they were unlike any beds that Goldilocks had ever seen! They were really piles of straw and leaves and pine needles and bird feathers, each pile covered with a fuzzy blanket.

What sort of family would sleep this way?
Goldilocks wondered.

She climbed onto the largest pile and found that it was made of mostly pine needles and was very hard and prickly.

Then she climbed onto the middle pile, made mostly of duck feathers, and found it much too puffy and soft.

The third pile was the smallest, with a wooly blanket
her own size, and this bed she found quite comfortable.
She settled down with a sigh. *I will only shut my eyes for a
wee moment,* she thought—but before her next breath,
she was sound asleep.

Meanwhile, three brown bears came lumbering back from a walk they had taken while their porridge cooled. When they saw the pile of sweepings outside the door of their cabin, Papa Bear let out a roar. "Who has come and made a mess of our fine house?" he cried. He saw that their front door was slightly open. "Shhhh," he said to the others. "We must go inside and look for clues."

The three bears all came inside fearfully,
with Papa Bear leading the way, sniffing the
air and rolling his bearish head.

When they came to the hearth,
the three bears saw at once what had
happened to their breakfast. Mama Bear
cried, "Who has come inside and ruined
my perfect porridge?"

Baby Bear came up behind her and peered into his empty bowl. "Someone first ruined my porridge and *then* used all my honey and *then* ate every last bite!" And he began to snuffle and cry.

"Shhhh," Papa Bear said.
"We must look for other clues."

He lumbered through the cabin, baring his teeth, Mama and Baby Bear close behind him. When he came upon his bed, he saw that his blanket was rumpled. "Someone has come in and mussed my kingly bed!" he cried.

Mama Bear saw that her pile had sunk down and her blanket was also mussed. "Someone has come in and mussed my queenly bed, too!" she exclaimed.

Baby Bear crouched over his own bed and he spoke in a voice that was more surprised than angry. "Someone has come in and mussed my bed," he gasped. "And look, Mama—here she very much still is!"

The three bears came closer to look in amazement at the sleeping Goldilocks. "Poor creature," said Papa Bear. "She has no soft fur but that odd patch on her head."

"Poor creature," said Mama Bear. "She has no lovely claws for catching fish in the river."

"Poor creature," said Baby Bear. "Her teeth are so small and silly."

They all three stared down at Goldilocks.

At that very moment, Goldilocks woke from her nap and opened her eyes. Only inches away were the furry snouts and sharp teeth of the bears. She was too afraid even to blink. Behind the bears, she spied a window open just enough for a little person to squeeze through. She jumped from the bed, dashed to the window, and wiggled through in a flash.

Then she ran and ran and ran, all the way back to her own house, where her father was setting the table.

He asked, "Did you remember my advice today, child?"

Goldilocks was still out of breath from running, and she gasped, "Yes, Papa, I must never, ever, *ever* go headlong into a cabin in the woods full of bears!"

"That is not exactly what I said," said her father, "but it is worth remembering."

The End